Mimi and Momoy

Kids' Adventure Begin

BY

FRANZ HIBMA

Copyright © 2023 **Franz Hibma Publishing**

All rights reserved. No part of this publication may be reproduced, distributed, or transmitted in any form or by any means, including photocopying, recording, or other electronic or mechanical methods, without the prior written permission of the publisher, except in the case of brief quotations embodied in critical reviews and certain other noncommercial uses permitted by copyright law. For permission requests, write to the publisher, addressed "Attention: Book Rights and Permission," at the address below.

Published in the United States of America

ISBN 978-1-962730-64-8 (HC)

Franz Hibma Publishing
Calgary Alberta Canada
www.stellarliterary.com

Order Information and Rights Permission:

Quantity sales. Special discounts might be available on quantity purchases by corporations, associations, and others. For details, contact the publisher at the address above.

For Book Rights Adaptation and other Rights Permission.
Call us at toll-free 1-888-945-8513 or send us an email at
admin@stellarliterary.com.

Mimi is a kid who lives in North America with her parents that is originally from the Philippines. She always have her slingy clingy sling bag friend (kaibigan) "BEARLY" with her. BEARLY is one of her best friends.

Mimi is a very smart 5-year-old girl and friendly. She loves helping her Mommy Linda doing chores inside their home.

One day she asked her mom. "Mom what are you cooking today?"

"I will cook one of your favorite food today, Mimi!" says Mommy Linda. "We will cook sopas (soup)!"

"Wow! Mommy thank you so much, my little tummy will be happy again. Can I help you Mommy in the kitchen?" says Mimi.

"Yes you can, Mimi. For sure!" says Mommy Linda.

Momoy is a boy who lives in North America with his parents originally from the Philippines. He loves adventure and dancing.

He have his "sombrero" hat friend (kaibigan) "BENTOY" everytime with him. He loves wearing it.

He also have his friendly playful dog "PIPO".

Momoy's Mom and Dad is so happy to see him growing as kind and active boy (bata).

One day Momoy is ready for the day to start playing in their backyard with PIPO the dog. He saw his dad doing some gardening.

"Dad can I help you?" Asked Momoy.

Dad says, "Thank you, Momoy. Yes you can just hand me that bucket (timba) and you can continue playing with "PIPO".

"Okay Dad!" (tatay).

1) Who is Mimi?

2) What is the name of her favorite sling bag?

3) Who is Momoy?

4) What is the name of his favorite friendly hat?

5) What is the name of his friendly dog?

Printed by Libri Plureos GmbH in Hamburg, Germany